JP
HOW

Howard, Ellen.

The big seed.

$14.00

DATE			

The Big Seed

The Big Seed

by Ellen Howard
illustrated by Lillian Hoban

SIMON & SCHUSTER BOOKS FOR YOUNG READERS
Published by Simon & Schuster
New York   London   Toronto   Sydney   Tokyo   Singapore

SIMON & SCHUSTER BOOKS FOR YOUNG READERS
Simon & Schuster Building, Rockefeller Center
1230 Avenue of the Americas, New York, New York 10020.
Text copyright © 1993 by Ellen Howard.
Illustrations copyright © 1993 by Lillian Hoban.
All rights reserved including the right of reproduction
in whole or in part in any form.
SIMON & SCHUSTER BOOKS FOR YOUNG READERS
is a trademark of Simon & Schuster.
Designed by Vicki Kalajian.
The text of this book is set in 14 pt Aster.
The illustrations were done in watercolor and color pencils.
Manufactured in the United States of America
10 9 8 7 6 5 4 3 2 1
Library of Congress Cataloging-in-Publication Data
Howard, Ellen. The big seed / by Ellen Howard;
illustrated by Lillian Hoban. Summary: As her mystery seed
develops throughout the summer, Bess discovers growing
makes things just the right size. [1. Size—Fiction.]
I. Hoban, Lillian, ill. II. Title. PZ7.H83274Bi
1992 [E]—dc20 CIP 91-19128
ISBN 0-671-73956-5

Many thanks to the Portland "groups"
who heard this, and heard this,
and heard this tirelessly.

To Beth and Chuck
EH

Bess was the smallest child in her class. No one was smaller. Not one boy. Not one girl. When everyone crowded around the big table, Bess was too small to see over their heads.

One day, Ms. Gilligan said that spring was coming. "It is time to choose seeds to plant," she said.

Bill shoved in front of Bess at the table. "Out of my way," said Bill.

Pearl jostled Bess with her round, dimpled elbow. "I want radish seeds," said Pearl.

"No fair!" said Bess.

Ms. Gilligan was telling about the seeds, but Bess didn't listen. She ran to her and pulled on her arm. "No fair!" said Bess. "I always have to go last."

"There are plenty of seeds," said Ms. Gilligan. "What kind of seeds do you want?"

Bess looked at the piles of seeds on the table. Beside each pile was a bright seed packet.

One packet showed carrots, big and orange, as long and thin as Bill. Bill was taking carrot seeds, which were tiny and flat.

The second seed packet showed big red radishes, as plump and round as Pearl. Pearl was taking radish seeds, which were little.

The third seed packet showed yellow flowers. They looked small like Bess, but the seeds were big.

"I want this kind," said Bess. She took a big seed.
Bess planted her seed in a cut-off milk carton.
She put it by the window, where the sun would
make it warm.

At home, Bess told her family, "I planted a seed."
"That's nice, dear," said Mother. "Take off your
boots before you walk on the rug."

"Big deal," said Cindy, Bess's big sister.

But her stepfather, Charlie, put down his book. "What kind of seed?" he asked.

"A *big* seed," said Bess.

"What will grow from it?" said Charlie.

Bess thought and thought.

She hadn't been listening when Ms. Gilligan was talking, but she remembered the seed packet picture.

"Small yellow flowers," she said.

"Marigolds?" Charlie said.

That sounded right to Bess. "Yes, marigolds," she said.

Outside, the sun shone
more and more often.
The daffodils bloomed.
The grass grew green.

In the classroom, Bess and her classmates
watered their seeds whenever the soil was dry.

"What are you growing, Bess?" said Bill.

"Yellow flowers," said Bess.

One day, a little green shoot poked out of the soil in Bess's milk carton. A little green shoot poked out of the soil in Pearl's carton, too.

"Look how my radish is growing," said Pearl.

"My flower is growing, too," said Bess. "It's bigger than your radish."

Bess wondered about that. "Are small yellow flowers supposed to be bigger than big red radishes?" she asked Ms. Gilligan.

But Ms. Gilligan was handing out work sheets.

"It is time for spelling, Bess," she said. "Go sit down in your seat."

Some milk cartons
had two little plants. Some
milk cartons had three.
Bess had only one plant,
but it was big.

The plants sprouted leaves.

Bess and her classmates turned the milk cartons
every day so the plants would grow straight. Bess's
plant was the biggest of them all.

"Are small yellow flowers big at first?" asked Bess.

But Ms. Gilligan was
saying they should take
their plants home. "Put
them in your gardens,"
she said.
"Summer is coming, and
school will soon be out."

Bess took her milk carton home. "I have to put my plant in the garden," Bess told her mother.

"That's nice, dear," said Mother. "But right now I need you to try on these pants."

"I have to put my plant in the garden," Bess told Cindy.

"Good," said Cindy. "That'll keep you out of my hair for a while."

"I have to put my plant in the garden," Bess told Charlie.

"Your marigold?" Charlie said. "Well, the trowel and the watering can are in the shed."

So Bess took her milk carton out to the garden.

She dug a hole with the trowel. She put the plant in the hole. She patted the soil around the plant. She sprinkled it with water.

Every summer day the sun shone on Bess's plant. Every day she watered it.

The plant grew.

"My marigold is getting big," said Bess.

"That's nice, dear," said Mother.

"So what?" said Cindy.

"You must be taking good care of it," Charlie said.

And the plant grew.

"I think my marigold is getting too big," said Bess.

"Oh, I shouldn't think so, dear," said Mother.

"Ummm," said Cindy.

"I'll come in a while to see," Charlie said.

But he forgot.

And the plant grew.

"How big is a marigold before it blooms?" Bess asked her mother.

"Not very big," said Mother. "Don't worry, dear."

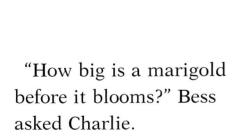

"How big is a marigold before it blooms?" Bess asked Cindy.

"How should I know?" said Cindy.

"How big is a marigold before it blooms?" Bess asked Charlie.

"Why don't we go take a look at it?" Charlie said.

Out in the garden, Charlie looked at Bess's plant.
"My marigold is very big," said Bess, feeling worried.
She saw that a smile was pulling Charlie's
mouth lopsided.

"It *is* big," said Charlie.

"Is it TOO big?" said Bess.

"It's too big for a marigold, Bess," Charlie said, "but if it is a *sunflower*, it is just the right size."

"A sunflower?" Bess said, surprised.

"Yes," said Charlie, "and your sunflower's blossom will make seeds for the birds."

Bess thought about birds eating seeds her flower had made. She began to smile.

Outside, the days were getting cool. The grass turned yellow. The leaves turned red.

Inside, Mother got out Bess's school clothes.

"Autumn is coming," she said. "We'll have to go shopping. You've grown too big for these clothes."

"Too big?" said Bess. "I'm not too big. I'm too small."

"Why, Bess," said Mother, "you're not too small."

"I'm shorter than Bill," said Bess. "I'm skinnier than Pearl."

"That's true," Mother said, "but you are not Bill, and you are not Pearl. You are our own dear Bess."

On the first day of school, Bill and Pearl came by Bess's house to walk with her. They, too, had grown bigger.

She took them to the garden. "See my sunflower," said Bess.

"It sure grew tall," said Bill. "It's taller than me, and I'm TOO tall."

"Its blossom is rounder than me," said Pearl, "and I'm TOO round."

"You're not too tall," Bess said to Bill.

"You're not too round," she said to Pearl.

"And I'm not too small, either.
I'm just the *right* size for me!"